we are champions

'brilliantly chosen by Wendy Cooling ... all are gripping, and offer real substance ... Each is a ray of sunshine for parents who are gloomy about the cost of encouraging their children to read. It's worth investing in the set.'

we are champions

stories chosen by
Wendy Cooling

Dolphin

A Dolphin Paperback
First published in Great Britain in 1997
by Orion Children's Books
a division of the Orion Publishing Group Ltd
Orion House
5 Upper St Martin's Lane
London WC2H 9EA

A catalogue record for this book is available
from the British Library

Typeset by Deltatype Ltd, Birkenhead, Merseyside
Printed in Great Britain by Clays Ltd, St Ives plc

Contents

Special

Alan Gibbons

Mrs Donnelly says I'm special,' said Roy. Only the way he said it told his mother special was a dirty word.

'That's good, isn't it?' she asked. But her voice had that little nervous shake that said she knew exactly what he was getting at.

'So how come I'm only special when I get taken out to read?'

At eleven o'clock every weekday morning Roy hated being special. Just hated it. That was when he had to collect his reading folder and sit at a table in the corridor with Mr Roberts. That was when he had to labour over the baby books they gave him, chewing over every word in the divvy stories about pigs that could talk and ducks that wore dresses. And what ten-year-old wants to read stuff like that?

'Sound it out,' Mr Roberts would say when Roy got stuck. And he got stuck a lot.

Sound it out yourself, Roy would think. Who cared if it was Percy or Penny Pig who wanted to cross the bumpety bridge? He would gladly have laid the dynamite that would have blown that stupid bumpety bridge to smithereens.

'You know what special means?' Roy asked. 'Thick, that's what. Everybody stares at me when I'm in the corridor.'

'Well, you're special to me,' said Mum, wincing

visibly at the word *thick*. 'Now get out there and prove it.'

Roy glanced at his team-mates jogging on to the pitch. He'd prove it, all right. Footy was something he was good at, always had been. In fact, it was his ability with the ball that saved him from the skitting some of the other kids in Mr Roberts' group got.

'You ready, Roy?' Marty Collins called. Marty was the skipper of Gilmoss Rovers.

'Coming.'

'Play a blinder, son,' said Mum.

He did too, tackling hard in defence and making some strong forward runs through the opposition defence. He might be a wing back and supposedly a member of the Rovers' back four, but he was their second highest scorer. He felt great. Strong, quick, *special*.

His chance to be really special came when Marty knocked an early ball across. Roy came in like a train, but he was ever so slightly behind the play. Throwing himself at the ball, he could only meet it with a glancing header. As the ball flew high over the bar, there were howls of derision from the opposition, and groans from his own side.

'Wasted that one, didn't you Woy?' said Marty. He said it as a joke, but Roy recognized the prickly, impatient tone of his voice. He thought Roy should have got to it. Roy could only glare at his captain and fume. *Woy*! It was a nickname that came back to haunt him every time he messed up. Woy of the Wovers. All because of the stupid lisp he used to have when he was in the infants. Nobody would ever let him forget it, especially the time when he went up to the teacher and told her: 'I wuv you.' It was really unfair. Why did Marty have to skit him over it all the time? They were supposed to be mates, weren't they? And you don't skit mates. But Roy stood out. He was the sort of mate you just had to tease. He was a special mate.

Marty must have seen the hurt look on Roy's face, because he immediately chipped in with another comment. 'Better luck next time, eh?'

Roy gave him a grateful smile. 'Yes, better luck next time.'

Next time wasn't long coming. Billy Mac connected with a long clearance downfield and took it route one into the opposition goalmouth. A cool lay-off and he'd put Roy clear. Just a tap-in really. 1–0. Mum was cheering on the touch-line and giving him the thumbs up.

Roy was really motoring after that. A goal just before half-time and his hat-trick completed just after. There were goals by Billy Mac and Marty in between, giving the Rovers a 5–0 win.

'That was great,' said Mum as they got in the car. 'You should feel proud of yourself. You are special.'

Then the car radio started to play. *Three lions*. Not the best song in the world, but it still made him smile. Music always helped.

He gave Mum a smile. 'Special eh? Yes, maybe.'

Monday morning, eleven o'clock and he was back out in the corridor with Mr Roberts. Failing. Roy chewed over the memory of Sunday's 5–0 victory like old chewing gum, but the flavour had faded already. He might be a winner on the football field but here in school he was the world's number one loser. While Mr Roberts sorted the various sheets he carried about in his battered briefcase, Roy inspected his new book: *Cassie Cat goes to Sea.*

'Ready then, young man?' said Mr Roberts breezily, clicking his ballpoint pen.

'Yes, whatever,' grunted Roy. He hadn't even turned the cover, yet he hated Cassie Cat. Hated her with a vengeance.

'Good.' Mr Roberts was going to ignore Roy's surly answer. 'Read me the title.'

Roy had worked it out. *Cassie* had stumped him at first. It was a hard word, but weren't they all? Roy hated words, hated them because they scared him. If reading was as important as everybody said, why did it have to be so rotten hard?

'Something cat goes to sea,' he said.

'And what's the something?'

'Dunno.'

'Then try sounding it out. You know *c-a-*, don't you?'

'Yeah, ca.'

'Add an *s* sound.'

'Cass.'

'Now -*ie*. Remember, we've done this. It's like a *y* at the end of the word.'

'Cassie.'

Mr Roberts beamed. Roy didn't return the smile. You think you've taught me something, he thought. Well, you never, because I knew it already.

'Good lad,' said Mr Roberts. 'Read on.'

It had been a slow start, and it got worse. Roy toiled over nearly every word. Soon his neck was burning with shame and embarrassment, and every time Mr Roberts tried to help, it just made things worse. Reading was hard and nothing anybody did was going to make it any easier.

Roy's suffering was finally brought to an end when Mr Roberts glanced at his watch. 'Oh well, time's up, Roy. I've got to fit Jennifer in before lunch.'

Roy slipped gratefully into class and dropped into his seat next to Marty. Whenever Roy went out with Mr Roberts, Marty had to brief him on what the class had been doing. That's why his teacher Mrs Fay didn't mind them talking.

'Heard who we've got in the first round of the Cup?' asked Marty.

'No, who?'

'Only Clubmoor Colts.'

'But we play them this Sunday in the league.'

'That's what I'm telling you. We're playing them

twice in a fortnight, first in the league, then in the Cup.'

'Bit of a coincidence, isn't it?'

Marty shrugged his shoulders. 'It happens.'

Roy was about to say something else when Mrs Fay looked across at them.

'Marty Collins,' she said. 'Are you quite sure you're discussing the Spartan army?'

Roy stared down at his worksheet. There was a picture of a half-naked bloke with a funny hat and a sword.

'The what?'

'Spartans,' Marty said loudly for Mrs Fay's benefit. 'Bunch of Greek fellers. Rock hard.'

Roy was interested, but only for a few moments. When he couldn't make head nor tail of the library book Marty passed him, he copied a couple of sentences off him and stared out of the window. Reading was hard. As in impossible.

Devastated. That was the only word for Roy's mood the following Sunday morning at final whistle. Clubmoor hadn't just beaten Rovers: they'd taken them to the cleaners. What hurt was that they'd done it by completely dominating the Rovers down the right flank, and that was Roy's patch. There was this kid playing for Clubmoor, Kieran McCann, and he'd had the beating of Roy right from the kick-off. McCann had come off the blocks like he meant to prove something. He did too. He proved that Roy wasn't so special on the pitch, after all. As he sat on the touch-line, arms hugging his knees, head sagging, he relived every minute of their one-sided duel.

It started badly when McCann turned him inside-out in the first minute, going round the outside to whip in the cross that lead to Clubmoor's opening goal. Then it got worse. A lot worse. Three of Clubmoor's first-half goals came from right-sided crosses, and that was down to Roy's inability to stop McCann. The Rovers rallied a bit in the second-half and their better form took some of the pressure off Roy. It didn't prevent one last act of humiliation, though. In the last minute Clubmoor were leading 7–2 and McCann picked the ball up on the half-way line. The moment he started his run, Roy was backing off. He had a lump in his throat. He was going to get taken again, and everybody was watching.

'Get into him, Roy,' yelled Marty.

But Roy's bottle had gone. He backed off and backed off and that's when it happened. Right in front of goal he slipped and fell. Smack on his backside. McCann gave a triumphant grin and ran on to slot home his side's eighth goal.

'Well, you certainly got into him,' said Marty. '*Woy!*'

With that, the skipper had stormed off. Roy felt the bitter taste of defeat in his mouth. Sure, they'd lost before, but never this heavily. For the first time he had to come to terms with a cruel truth. Even on the pitch there were kids who could play better. Loads of them. Even there he wasn't special.

It was nearly a week before Roy started to get over it. Saturday night to be exact, the eve of their re-match with Clubmoor. Music helped. As usual. And it was a football anthem that did it. As usual. Roy sat in his room brooding over the 8–2 thrashing and listening to the radio. That's when it came on. *You'll Never Walk Alone*. He heard the piano playing a rhythm like falling rain and the singer's voice, sad and soft like the wind off the Mersey, driving out the words that had hoisted a million football scarves.

That's right, that's what he'd do: walk on, fight on. There was always another day.

Roy started to smile. He wouldn't be afraid of the dark, he wouldn't be afraid of anything. Who did this McCann lad think he was anyway? He was only another snotty-nosed kid from the North End. It's not like he was Robbie Fowler or Steve McManaman or something. He'd had a good day. Maybe on Sunday it would be Roy's turn to shine.

Too right! And this time there was going to be a golden sky, his golden sky. His! Suddenly Roy was laughing as if all eight goals they'd let in had been flukes.

'You sound happy,' said Mum poking her head round the door.

'Yes,' said Roy as the song's last drumbeat died away. 'That's because I am.'

The strain on Roy's face must have been showing because Marty came up to him at half-time.

'Everything all right?' he asked.

'Yes, why shouldn't it be?'

Roy's reply was a fierce challenge. He'd kept McCann at bay, hadn't he? It hadn't been easy, either. Roy knew the leggy Clubmoor player had the beating of him if he wasn't on his game. But he'd kept at it, bumping, pushing, crowding, never giving his opponent an inch. He'd stuck to his man like a limpet.

'I was only asking,' said Marty, taken aback. 'You've been sound.'

'Yes,' said Roy flatly. He wasn't taking any flannel off Marty. One slip and he'd be getting the *Woy* treatment again. 'I know.'

He was better than all right in the second half. His marking had demoralised McCann and he was able to make a few forward runs of his own. They didn't come to anything though, and the teams were stalemated at 0–0.

'Something's got to give,' said Marty. 'I can't take the tension.'

'Something *did* give. It was Marty. He was trying to work the ball out of defence when he gave the ball away. To McCann of all people! The Clubmoor winger had been fading, but suddenly he saw his chance to be a hero. A moment after intercepting Marty's sloppy ball, he was bearing down on Roy. Go past him and he would have the goal at his mercy.

'Get into him!' came the cries of Roy's team-mates.

Roy's heart was crawling into his mouth. All the time McCann was driving forward they were staring at each other. This was the final showdown. Roy watched the jinking run and he was afraid. Scared witless of McCann's pace. He held off and held off, expecting McCann to make his break. When it came, the drive into the box was unstoppable. McCann pushed the ball and flashed past.

'No-o-o,' came the voices of his team mates.

The Rovers might have given up, but not Roy. McCann was past him and into the penalty area. Roy's tackle had to be inch-perfect. Turning, he steadied himself. He remembered the strains of *You'll Never Walk Alone*. This time, it wasn't on the radio. It was in his head.

He didn't give up. He hoped. He dared. Keeping his eye on the ball, he propelled himself forward.

He slid across the greasy turf. The ball had sat up for McCann and Roy made contact. For a second he winced. Touch the man and it was a penalty. But his boot met the ball. Clean as a whistle. Then Chris, their goalie was in attendance. Grinning gratefully at Roy, he dribbled it out of harm's way. In an instant Roy was running forward to give Chris a target.

'Mine!' he bawled.

Chris wasn't about to refuse him. Gathering the ball on the edge of the area, Roy powered forward. He was on fire. Beating two opponents by sheer pace, he had carved an opening for himself.

'Roy,' yelled Marty, peeling away to the left. 'First time ball.'

Roy released it and Marty did the business with the crisp, square pass. They'd done it. 1–0. The moment the whistle went, Roy was mobbed. Up against a far better player he'd stuck to his guns and come through. He was so high he started to do something he'd only ever done in the privacy of his own room. He actually started to sing. *You'll never walk alone.* That's when he noticed everyone staring. Like he was doing something special.

Just how special he found out a couple of weeks later. It was their class assembly and Mr Roberts had got him to sing. For the whole school! He felt a divvy at first. For a start, Mum was in the front row. And that's not all. Some of the kids were pointing, others were laughing. But the moment Roy started to sing, the entire hall fell silent. Three hundred kids and not a murmur. And at the end there was this long silence, then applause. Loads of it. Like heavy rain.

'That was amazing,' said Marty afterwards. 'Mr Roberts says you've got a gift.'

'It's not so special,' said Roy. 'It's easy.'

Funnily enough, Roy was saying the same thing to Mr Roberts at eleven o'clock that morning. This time he wasn't talking about singing. He meant his book.

'So what's the cat called?' asked Mr Roberts.

'Cassie,' Roy answered. 'Stupid name for a cat.'

'I agree,' said Mr Roberts. 'We'll try reading some football magazines next week.'

'I'd like that,' said Roy. 'Reading's easy.'

It wasn't, but somehow it was never quite so difficult again.

The Secret
Weapon

Sam Jackson

t's 7–6!'

'More like 6 all!'

'Look.' Simon put his hands on his waist and glared at Joanne. 'I'm the one keeping score. We had a penalty, remember?'

Jo flashed him an impish smile.

'Which you *missed*, Si!' She ran a hand through her short black hair and peered at Simon with dark eyes.

'Oh ... errr,' Simon shrugged as the rest of the lunch-time football crew gathered around. 'But we had another one!' he said excitedly. 'I blasted it past Ryan!'

Jo recalled Simon's stocky frame belting the ball towards goal. Ryan had stood still in the goal, like a Subbuteo figure with his arms poised for a catch. He had stayed still as the ball whisked past his ear, not moving until it had bounced off the mesh fence and walloped him on the back of the head.

Short and cheeky, Ryan was Joanne's best friend, the first year's classroom entertainer. His antics usually had everyone cracking up at least once during the frantic lunch-hour game up on the tennis courts.

'Well, I think we all remember that one,' Jo said with a chuckle. She gave Ryan a quick dig in the ribs. 'But it's still 6 all, Si.'

Jo sighed. It was the same every lunch-time. About five minutes before the afternoon bell was due to ring out across the courts and playing fields, Simon would become anxious that his team wasn't winning and would try to make out they were one or two up. Jo and Ryan were used to it, but they wished that Simon could just coolly lose the odd game without getting into such a flap. Since he'd been made captain of the first year Sandycliffe High team, he'd become fiercely competitive.

Arguing with Simon was pretty pointless. Jo and Ryan liked to wind him up if they could. His pale blue eyes would grow wide and serious and his shock of ginger hair trembled as he tried to get his point across. Ryan squatted down and began imitating the actions of a large flapping bird about to take off.

Simon ignored him. 'Ask Matt,' he yelled.

Matt Dean was over by the steps on what Jo thought must be his eightieth keep-up, in a world of his own with his precious Adidas ball. Gorgeous Matt Dean, tall and blue-eyed, was Sandycliffe's top goalscorer and master skillsman.

'Hey! David Beckham!' Ryan yelled to him. 'What's the score?'

Matt glanced distractedly towards the group. '6 all.'

Simon threw Matt a murderous look as the others burst out laughing.

'Let's show him,' Ryan said to Jo before jogging off towards his goal.

They started again from the centre. The lunch-time games on the courts were always frantic and Jo's legs were never free of colourful bruises. Simon was good at dishing them out, the way he blundered in at anyone who had possession. But this time Jo nudged the ball left as Simon came thundering towards her. Suddenly Ryan came streaking into the attacking third. Jo touched the ball into his path as he powered through the defence and fired a shot through the middle of the bag markers.

He threw his arms up in an exaggerated celebration. 'Peter Schmeichel eat your heart out! 7–6 to us!'

'Nice one!' Jo told him as they headed in for afternoon lessons.

'Great pass from our lunch-time guest star!' Ryan said, in the style of John Motson. 'If I were Captain I'd let you in the school team. You'd easily make it if we picked the best eleven. Simon's such a wally not letting you in. Mr Shaw shouldn't leave it up to him anyway.'

Ryan grinned cheekily. 'You could play up front with Matt,' he said with a wink and proceeded to break into song. 'Because heeeeee's gorgeous!'

Jo shoved him away playfully.

'I'm not bothered really,' she said. 'It's just knowing that Simon and some of the others won't have me in the real team … It just makes me more determined. Just one chance is all I want.'

'Mr Shaw said they're mad not to have you,' Ryan said.

Jo stared at him. 'No kidding!'

Simon jogged up alongside them. 'Matt said he made a mistake earlier with the scores so I guess your effort made it seven all.'

Ryan looked at Jo and shook his head. He placed a sympathetic arm around Simon's shoulders and spoke in his ear in low, soothing tones. 'Si, it really is okay to lose the lunch-time game. You're not going to get suspended or anything.'

Simon tutted and walked off towards the science labs.

Jo glanced up at the main block and saw Mr Chambers glaring down at them from the first floor maths room, where she and Ryan were due two minutes ago.

'Oh-oh,' said Ryan. The two of them sprinted to the double doors.

Jo sat in her usual place, next to Nikki at the back of the classroom. Bubbly Nikki Grainger was in trouble almost every lesson for talking and giggling. With Ryan on her other side, Jo wondered whether she should perhaps move if she was to have any hope of getting a half decent maths report this year. It was difficult trying to concentrate on Mr Chambers, standing by the blackboard barking algebra examples, with Nikki whispering ridiculous questions about Matt Dean every ten seconds.

When Mr Chambers began rummaging in his desk Jo turned to her. 'For the millionth time, Nikki. I play footie with the lads at lunch because I enjoy it, not because I want to be near Matt. Okay! If you like him so much, why don't you join us?'

'Oh, I couldn't,' Nikki said quickly, fiddling with a long strand of wavy blonde hair. 'I'd be useless.'

Ryan leaned across Jo. 'You're dead right there,' he said flatly.

Nikki lurched at Ryan with her ruler, hitting his hand with several loud slapping noises. Jo wasn't surprised to look up and discover that they had attracted the attention of the stern maths teacher.

Ryan spoke into Jo's ear while trying to wrestle the ruler from Nikki's determined grasp. 'I reckon you should turn up to our practice tomorrow.'

Jo shook her head.

'Okay then,' Ryan went on. 'Your netball practice is tonight, yeah?'

Jo turned to him sharply.

Ryan had time to grin and say, 'I'll see you there then,' before his name was bellowed from the front of the classroom.

'Nikki must hold the record for getting sent out of Chambers' class!' Jo said to her friend Lucy as she finished fastening her red games skirt, 'And Ryan was ordered to sit on the front row with the boffins for the next fortnight.'

Lucy gathered her thick brown hair into a high bunch.

'Why *don't* you go to the practice like Ryan suggested?' she asked Jo. 'The others wouldn't mind.'

Jo sighed. 'I don't reckon they want to be seen to go against Simon, whatever his problem is. He'd really flip if he thought they were all against him.'

Miss Irving handed Jo a net full of orange netballs as the girls passed her on the way out of the P.E. corridor. 'Be with you in a minute, girls,' she said.

It was ten minutes later when Miss Irving strolled towards the courts, and Ryan was beside her, dressed in tracky bottoms and trainers.

'What on *earth* is he doing?' Lucy spluttered.

Jo eyed the approaching duo suspiciously. She pulled a face. 'I don't think I want to find out.'

'Right, girls!' said Miss Irving as the curious netball squad gathered round. 'We have a new recruit today. I'm not sure whether Ryan has any real intention of representing Sandycliffe at netball . . . But as you know, everyone is welcome to have a go. So, Ryan,' she turned to the surprise guest who was trying to hide an idiotic grin. 'Are you familiar with the rules of the game?'

Ryan smiled confidently. 'Not a clue, miss! But I'm eager to learn.'

'Fine!' Miss Irving looked at him with a slightly

glazed expression. Jo felt herself cringing as a giggle rippled around the group. 'Lucy and Jo will fill you in.'

Jo dragged Ryan away from the group.

'You're off your trolley if you think this is going to make me go to footy practice,' she whispered to Ryan sternly.

Ryan shrugged, plainly enjoying the stir he was causing.

'Irving was cool about it,' he said cheerfully. 'I should have a laugh, looks easy enough. Like basketball, but duller, yeah?'

Lucy let out a wicked laugh. 'Just you wait,' she said.

Miss Irving handed Ryan the Goal Attack bib for the practice game, and with a glint in her eye promptly organised Deborah Burdett as the opposing Goal Defence to mark him. If there was one person, Jo thought, who *wouldn't* be amused at Ryan turning up it was Deborah – the Simon of the netball crew. Tall and hefty, Deborah towered over Ryan as they stood side by side, poised for the whistle.

From the outset Deborah stuck to Ryan like a giant limpet. Jo watched as his fixed grin slowly settled into an angry grimace as he battled with his marker. Lucy giggled throughout the action. Jo was loving it as well. Seeing her laugh-a-minute friend becoming more furious by the moment was a treat. When Ryan did manage to snatch a pass, Deborah arrived like a giant spider in front of him, waving her arms around to cover any direction he might pass the ball.

Ryan managed one shooting chance after twenty minutes. As he held the ball aloft, sizing up the shot, determination etched on his face, Deborah settled into her defensive stance, balancing on one leg and leaning in like a huge crane to place a broad palm two inches from the ball. Ryan teased her with a mischievous grin and moved the ball from side to side. As Deborah wobbled, Ryan hurled the ball. It crashed against the high fence five yards behind the ring to an outburst of hysterical laughter. It all ended abruptly when the cheeky pretender received a stiff elbow to the chin. Deborah did an expert job at making it look like an accident.

'I have to say,' Ryan said as they walked home, touching his jaw tenderly, 'that was one of the worst half hours of my life. Deborah Burdett is a nightmare. She's possessed!'

Lucy and Jo giggled.

'Like basketball but duller,' said Jo, mocking Ryan's earlier words.

'I'll be back!' he said dramatically.

'Hard luck about not making the team for the game against St Paul's,' Lucy teased.

Ryan turned to Jo.

'But the point is,' he said, sounding like a teacher, 'that if I *had* been good enough, I would have been picked. I made a total dork of myself to show you that you should forget about Simon and his "No Girls" rule and go for it!'

Jo looked at him. 'Thanks for making us all laugh, Ry, but we'll see.'

Thursday's lunch-hour game had been going a few seconds before Jo dodged past a defender to score. Ryan delivered a stinging congratulatory slap on the back. Lucy and Nikki were watching from the steps. Not the football, but Matt Dean. They clapped loudly when he sent a left-footed shot skidding across the concrete past Ryan.

Simon became stressed about the score at the usual time, but even *he* couldn't dream up four goals that didn't exist.

As they piled down the steps at the end of the lunch-hour, Lucy stood up, boldly blocking Simon's path.

'Si, how come you won't let Jo be in the team?' she asked coolly.

Simon smiled awkwardly. The gang gathered round and waited for his response. His cheeks flushed a deep red before he seemed to gather himself and slung his bag over his shoulder.

'Not good for our image,' he said flatly and walked away.

Nikki shouted after him. 'What *image*? We're useless!'

Simon didn't look round.

'He's got a mate who plays for St Paul's, Adam Bennett.' It was Matt who spoke.

Everyone leaned in closer, interested in this new revelation.

'Si said Bennett would never let him forget it if we had a girl playing for us.'

Apart from Lucy blurting her disgust, the news was received with a thoughtful silence.

Nikki gazed up at Matt. 'What do you think?'

Matt paused for a moment. 'I think Jo's good,' he said matter-of-factly. 'I wouldn't mind if I got more service up front.' He shrugged and suddenly, as if sensing the complete attention of the surrounding crowd, he strode away. Nikki almost fell flat on her face in a effort to gather up her bag and follow him.

'So. Simon's scared of looking like a wally in front of his little friend?' Ryan sneered.

'Bennett's totally rubbish!' Parmi said. 'He scored the worst own goal ever that time. He's the guy that always tries those stupid bicycle kicks.'

Ryan burst out laughing. 'No wonder he doesn't want us to get any better!'

Jo looked out across the fields as she headed for the school gates. Down on the bottom pitch the goals had been set out, ready for the evening football practice. Lucy's words during History still echoed around her head.

'The others want you,' Lucy had urged.

Jo sighed. It just wasn't her style to force her way

into anything. Simon would have to ask her. Rounding the corner, Jo almost collided with the broad figure of Mr Shaw.

'Sorry, I was miles away,' Jo said apologetically.

'Joining us?' the teacher asked with a broad smile. Jo shook her head.

'It'll be a tough one on Saturday against St Paul's. I'd love to show that games teacher of theirs we can do something.' Mr Shaw mused.

Jo sat in the shelter on Saturday morning and watched the double-decker bus sail past. Lucy was late again. Jo glanced at her watch. Half-eleven. Sandycliffe would be well into the second half of the game against St Paul's.

Jo looked up when she heard hurried footsteps. Expecting Lucy, she felt a shudder of surprise to see Matt jogging past. He spun round as she called his name. Matt looked stressed, yet he was clearly relieved to see Jo.

'Lifesaver!' he said breathlessly. 'Got to get my kit up to school for Mr Shaw . . . wants to send faulty shirts back after the game . . .'

Jo frowned at him. 'But why aren't you playing?'

Matt swallowed and began to speak more regularly. 'My brother set fire to our living-room, the little pain, just as I was about to set off. Mum thought he was old enough to be left on his own as well. Our neighbour is sitting with him while I take this up to the school, but he's going out so I can't be long. Will you do me a massive favour and take my kit to Mr Shaw?'

Jo took the handle of the heavy black bag.

'They must be playing with ten men,' said Matt. 'Andy couldn't make it either, I just saw him.'

Jo watched him dash away. She looked at her watch again. If she hurried, she would get to Sandycliffe just as the match was ending. An idea was beginning to take shape.

Lucy appeared by the shelter, her hair wild from the wind.

'I've got to get to the school,' Jo said urgently and she began to run.

Five minutes later she was beside Mr Shaw on the touch-line.

'Matt's kit,' she explained. The P.E. teacher thanked her distractedly, not taking his eyes away from the game. He told Jo the score was 1–0 to St Paul's. The match was nearly over.

'Turning up to play St Paul's with ten men!' Mr Shaw said angrily. 'Their man thinks we're a bunch of fools!'

Jo noticed the smug-looking rival coach.

The action was in the St Paul's penalty box. Jo glanced at Ryan, standing on the edge of his area. His hands in the huge keeper's gloves were frantically beckoning her. It was the last push Jo needed.

She threw away her heavy coat and began rummaging in Matt's bag. She pulled on the white number ten shirt over her plain top and the long, baggy shorts over black leggings. Her own suede trainers would have to do.

Mr Shaw hadn't noticed the frantic activity beside him. His eyes nearly popped out of his head when he turned and saw Jo ready to join the action. Without a word he signalled to the referee. Jo took a last glance around and saw Lucy thudding down the slope.

'Go for it!' she yelled and Jo ran on to the pitch feeling more nervous than she had ever felt in her whole life.

Of all the Sandycliffe team, Simon was the last to see Jo. A look of utter shock swept over his face as she sprinted towards the St Paul's area. Jo stood in front of him, waiting for instructions, but Simon just gawped. He glanced towards a fair-haired boy dressed in the dark red St Paul's strip. The boy was smiling slyly at Simon. Jo realised this must be Adam Bennett.

'Where do you want me?' Jo's shriek seemed to snap Simon out of his trance. 'We ... we've got a corner,' he stammered, then focused on Jo properly. 'You take it'.

Jo raced to the spot. Ryan had approached the half-way line. He was clapping his hands madly. 'Float one in,' he yelled.

Jo stood five paces back from the ball. 'Please don't let me hoof it behind the goal,' she whispered. As she took powerful strides into the shot, a sudden gust of wind lashed in towards the goal. The ball left

Jo's foot with a full, powerful contact – too far behind the waiting Sandycliffe trio of Simon, Parmi and Dave – until it began to curl in towards the crowd in the box.

Jo stood frozen to the spot. Parmi and Simon rose together towards the floating cross. Sandycliffe's two tallest players drew in the St Paul's defence. But at the last moment, a reverse gust whipped the ball away from its intended target. It passed by the scrambling bunch of players who had launched themselves towards the cross. But suddenly Ryan was there streaking up to the far post to slide the ball past St Paul's sprawling goalkeeper.

Ryan led the charge towards Jo with his usual two-armed celebration and Simon was right behind him.

'Wicked cross!' Simon shrieked.

Ryan and Jo were carried along amid hysterical whoops of delight from the rest of the team. Jo couldn't help noticing the mean stare Adam Bennett was giving Simon.

Ryan nudged him. 'Your mate looks mad,' he said.

But Simon didn't look bothered. 'No wonder,' he said, grinning broadly. 'He doesn't have a secret weapon, does he?'

The last minute went by in a complete whirl for Jo. She watched, dazed, as Bennett legged Simon over in the St Paul's area. The Sandycliffe captain blasted home the free shot to make it two-one to the home side. At the final whistle Mr Shaw looked almost delirious with delight. Lucy gave Jo a massive hug.

The Sandycliffe team walked away from the school still buzzing with excitement.

'Was one go enough, then?' Ryan asked Jo.

Jo looked round at them all. 'For now,' she said, unable to hide a huge grin. 'I can't take this kind of madness every Saturday!'

Top Striker

William Crouch

The new girl looked around at the supporters lining the pitch. Then she stared at the twenty-two players ready for the kick-off.

'This is weird, Rachel,' she said. 'Why don't they start? And where's the ball?'

'It's coming,' said Rachel. 'Listen!'

The sound was uncanny. Like a strong wind in a gale, thought Tasha. Or Mum's pressure cooker, or maybe someone letting air out of a giant-sized tyre.

Then she saw it. Behind the woods, on the other side of the field, was a huge blue blob. A massive hot-air balloon! The crew were hastily adding more gas to the tongue of flame in an effort to get over the trees.

'They've made it,' said Rachel. 'Now watch, Tasha.'

The balloon cleared the trees and dived low over the field. As it reached the pitch it seemed to hover. One of the crew leaned out of the basket and neatly dropped the ball into the centre circle.

'Wow!' said Tasha. 'You said Dale Valley Rovers had problems, Rache. Tell me about it. Do they do this every week?'

'Sort of,' said Rachel.

Tasha stared up as the balloon passed overhead. She read the catch-phrase painted in huge white letters: 'Blinks Butter Biscuits are Best.'

The ref positioned the ball and whistled the match into play. Danny, a Dale Valley striker, pushed the ball forward. Kev came from midfield to take it while Danny raced into Cowley Cobblers' half. Then, to everyone's amazement, Dale Valley's second striker ran for the ball. He collided with Kev, and both fell to the ground, Kev clutching his ankle and roaring at the striker. The ball was taken by a Cobblers' winger who lobbed it across to give his strikers time to get to the Dale Valley goal area. A clever pass from a Cobblers' midfielder gave the ball to a striker who, with perfect footwork, ran through the defenders and banged the ball into the net. Rob, the Dale Valley keeper, didn't stand a chance. Score: 1–0 after less than a minute's play!

'See what I mean?' said Rachel. 'We're in big trouble.'

'Pathetic,' agree Tasha. 'Who is that dimwit?'

'His name's Sidney Blinks. His dad's a millionaire and chairman of the youth club. Money's no problem. We've got everything: new buildings, gym, games room, playing field. And we've got Sidney. His dad insists that he's a striker.'

The two girls were joined by a group of Dale Valley supporters. The expressions on the kids' faces – utter misery and frustration – portrayed their opinion of Sidney Blinks.

'What can we do with him?' shouted Julie Jones.

'He's got to go,' muttered Andy Hugget. 'We must get rid of him.'

'Agreed,' said Rachel, 'but if Sidney goes, so does the club.' She took Tasha's arm. 'This is Tasha,' she said. 'Her family have just moved into Dale Valley. She's dead keen on football so I'm telling her the problem. Three yeas ago, Tasha, Dale Valley kids had nothing, not even a patch to bounce a ball on. Then Mr Johnnie Blinks, the world famous biscuit manufacturer, moved into the Manor House. He built the club and showered us with goodies.'

'Only because of his dear little Sidney,' shouted Julie.

'We all know that,' said Rachel. 'Don't yell at me, Julie. We're in this together.'

She was interrupted by a roar from the crowd. One of the Cobblers' strikers was hopping around in sheer agony and the ref was awarding a free kick. Sidney had done it again.

The group moved along the touchline to be nearer the action. The ball seemed to be permanently in Dale Valley's half and in the net far too often.

The score was now 5–0. Rob was in despair. He muttered, 'Not my fault,' when he saw Terry Bond, the coach and team manager, coming towards him.

'Don't worry,' said Terry. 'It'll be better next week.'

'You said that last week,' sighed Rob. 'It just gets worse. Mark and Trev were the best defenders we ever had. And they've left because they can't stand Sidney Blinks any longer.'

Terry knew the problem.

'Why don't you have girls in the team?' Tasha asked Rachel. 'I'd play.'

'So would I,' said Rachel. 'But Mr Blinks won't hear of it. He doesn't like girls.'

'Anyway,' said Sam Walker, the youngest and smallest supporter of Dale Valley Rovers, 'girls can't play football. Yuk!'

'I'll take you on any day,' said Tasha. 'Look, why don't we get a ball and have a kickabout under the trees?'

'Great!' said Rachel. 'Five-a-side?'

They borrowed a ball from Terry and made a couple of goals with their coats.

Tasha drew her long dark hair up over her head and fixed it with a hairband. She took the ball and headed it against the trunk of a tree. She kept this going, counting as she did so; stopping when she got to six. Then she juggled it on her knees, trapped it, dribbled it around Sam and Andy, just to show that girls are tops, and lobbed it over to Rachel.

She was surprised when Rachel neatly trapped it and booted it back to her.

'You're good, Rachel,' she said.

'Yeah,' said Rachel. 'Got three brothers. All football crazy. But where did you learn those tricks, Tasha?'

'Dad's a striker. He's just transferred to the Wanderers.'

'You mean Bigley Wanderers?'

'Yeah.'

'Phew! He must be good.'

Other kids came to watch. This was real football. Rachel and Tasha picked sides: a keeper, three midfielders and a striker.

Tasha was great. She scored a hat-trick within the first few minutes of the game. But then Rachel took Julie Jones out of goal and put in Sam. He had one ambition: to play as keeper for Dale Valley Rovers. Today he almost qualified. They finished the game 6–4.

'Tell you what,' said Andy, 'let's kick out silly Sidney and make Tasha our top striker. We'd murder the lot of 'em.'

Nobody spoke as they took their coats and made for the pitch. Then Julie Jones said: 'I've got an idea.'

'If it's the same as Andy's you know what to do with it,' said Rachel.

'Okay,' sighed Julie. 'But I think we should have a secret meeting.'

'Secret meeting? Where? What for?'

'We could have it in your dad's big shed. And talk about the team's problem. If we lose next week against Denby Flyers we might as well take up tiddlywinks or Junior Scrabble. It'll be nine defeats. One after the other.'

'Are you inviting Sidney and his dad?'

'Course not. Get real, Rache. We can't say what we like in the club because of Sidney. But if we have a secret meeting, someone may come up with an idea.'

Rachel considered this. Maybe Julie had a point. 'Okay. Ten o'clock tomorrow morning. I'll kick the word around.'

They were just in time to see Dale Valley's only goal. The game was still in the home team's half when Gary, in midfield, took the ball and fired it powerfully into the opposition's territory. Danny held it neatly, slipped past two defenders and slotted it home.

'13–1,' said Rachel. 'Could have been worse.'

'Yes,' agreed Tasha. 'So who's the striker? I'm impressed.'

The whole gang came to the meeting. The shed was massive; Rachel's dad had started his business there before moving to the industrial estate. Rachel banged on the table. 'Okay guys, let's get started. This is a proper meeting like we used to have before we got the club.'

'Before we got Sidney, you mean,' said Rob.

'Leave it out, Rob,' said Andy.

Rachel banged on the table again. 'Order!' she called. 'No more interruptions or I'll get Sam to throw you out.'

There was a guffaw but the gang settled down. There were plenty of seats. The shed was littered with empty wooden crates, a few broken chairs and a couple of ancient oak pews that had come from the church hall.

'This idea was Julie's,' said Rachel, 'so I'm going to ask her to begin the meeting. Over to you, Julie.'

'Well,' said Julie, 'we all moan about Sidney, but what do we do about it? Nothing.'

'What *can* we do?' said Rob.

'Shut up and listen!' snapped Julie. 'We've got to win next Saturday's match against the Flyers. We can do it if we haven't got Sidney and if Mark and Trev come back as defenders. Agreed?'

Most of the gang nodded.

'Mark, would you and Trev come back if we didn't play Sidney?' she asked.

'Yeah.'

'Good. Suggestions then on how to get rid of Sidney. Be serious.'

'Tie 'im up and put 'im in the river,' shouted Rob.

Julie was a first-class chairperson. She ignored Rob and went on. 'We've got to remember his dad always brings him to the match so we've got to take care of Mr Blinks as well.'

The gang came up with ideas. They were out of this world and quite impossible. Things like, tell him he's won the Lottery and will he go and collect the money on Saturday; Bigley wants him for their mascot but he must go to every match; Hollywood are making a film about kid's football and they want him to be the star.

They talked for over an hour and then Danny, who'd said nothing, put up his hand.

'Shush, you kids!' yelled Julie. 'Danny's got an idea. Over to you, Danny.'

'Okay,' said Danny. 'Sidney wants to make his name in football so let's put him on television.'

'How?'

'Saturday night's *Sports Quiz*. We get a message to Sidney and his dad just before the match starts saying that the Quiz want them to take part in that evening's show and will they come to the studio straight away for a rehearsal. They'll jump at it. By the time they find it's a hoax we'll have buried the Flyers. We'll have had Mark and Trev back as defenders and we'd have played a new striker.'

For a moment there was silence and then the gang began to hammer in the questions.

'Why wait until Saturday afternoon before giving them the invite?'

'Who's going to make the telephone call?'

'Who's the new striker?'

'Go on, Danny,' said Rachel. 'This is fantastic.'

'Okay,' said Danny. 'One at a time. If Mr Blinks gets a call before Saturday he's got plenty of time to find out it's a hoax. Agreed?'

There was a nodding of heads.

Danny went on. 'We'll get someone, perhaps Simon, Rachel's brother, to 'phone from the call box down the road. We'll give him a signal from the car park when they arrive.'

'Brilliant,' said Julie Jones. 'So who's our new striker, Danny?'

'She's sitting right here,' said Danny, putting his hand on Tasha's shoulder.

The next day Rachel and Julie went to see the club's coach. 'I hope it works,' Terry said, 'but don't count me in. When Mr Blinks finds out there'll be trouble and I don't want to lose my job.'

Simon was enthusiastic. 'Yeah. I'll make the call,' he said. 'I've never liked Johnnie Blinks or his sneaky little boy. I'll be at the call box and you can wave to me when he arrives. I'll chat him up and then invite him to the television studio.'

For the rest of the week they practised hard.

'You can't train with the team,' Danny told Tasha. 'Sidney might suspect something. But if you kick the ball around with Rachel and Sam I'll come along and give you a few tips.'

'Thanks, Danny,' said Tasha. She didn't mention that there might be some tips she could give him.

They trained in groups for dribbling and trapping; and in lines for spot kicks. Terry worked them hard in passing and positioning. Sidney came but watched for most of the time.

The gang knew that if their plan succeeded they stood a good chance of beating the Denby Flyers on Saturday. But after that . . ? 'Don't think about it,' said Rachel. 'It's worth the risk.'

Tasha sat in her mum's car. Her dad had gone to Bigley to play for the Wanderers so her mum had given her a lift to the Dale Valley game. She wore a red tracksuit over her football gear and the butterflies in her tummy were for real.

Rachel was at the entrance to the car park watching Simon. He was sitting on the bank at the side of the call box. Julie was in the club's office, keeping guard over the telephone.

Then the Rolls arrived. Mr Blinks drove into the car park as though he had royalty on the back seat. Rachel waved and saw Simon enter the box to make the call. Two minutes later, just as Mr Blinks was tying Sidney's trainers, Julie came running from the office.

'Sorry, Mr Blinks,' she said. 'A telephone call for you. The man says it's urgent. Something to do with Sidney.'

Mr Blinks ran into the club. Julie followed and listened at the office door.

'Yes, he's a good player and he knows a lot about the game,' he was saying. 'Rehearsal this afternoon and performance at 8.30 this evening? Good! I'll see you at the Bigley studio in about an hour.'

Mr Blinks stayed in the car park long enough to speak to the coach. 'Sorry, Terry,' he said. 'Sidney's been selected to appear on television. You'll have to find a replacement striker.'

Overhead a light aircraft swooped low across the pitch. It was towing a streamer that told everyone, in large red letters: 'Blinks Butter Biscuits are the Best.'

At the line-up Danny winked across at Tasha. 'We'll bury 'em,' he said.

But the Denby Flyers made a rapid start. Their midfield placed the ball in Dale Valley's half and, despite Mark's strong tackle, a striker ran clear to hammer the ball at the goal. It flew almost straight at Rob who fisted it brilliantly over the bar.

'We've got to get it in their half,' said Danny. He took the ball from Gary and raced towards the Flyer's goal. But their defenders closed in on him. He attempted to hook the ball to Tasha but he was too late. The ball was taken and booted back into Dale Valley's half.

Mark and Trev were on form. 'Good job we've got them back,' said Julie to Sam. He nodded. But the Flyers were desperate to get an early goal. Twice their strikers broke through Dale Valley's defence but each time Rob held the ball safely.

At half-time the score was 0–0.

'We're just not getting enough of the ball,' complained Tasha.

Terry agreed. 'Forget about fancy footwork,' he told the midfielders. 'Just keep booting long balls through the middle for our strikers to chase.'

This change in tactics surprised the Flyers' defenders. After a brilliant long ball from Kev in midfield Tasha took possession. She skirted around the defenders and hammered the ball into the corner of the net.

This was just the beginning of the best football Dale Valley had ever played. With powerful drives coming from their midfielders Tasha and Danny were getting a lot of the ball. The Flyers had put their strength into attacking but now, with Dale Valley on the offensive, they had to fall back and concentrate on their defence.

Tasha's second goal came from a brilliant header. A strong ball fired by Danny was returned to play by the Flyers' keeper. Tasha dived forward, cleverly avoiding a lunging defender, and placed the ball neatly over the line. Danny's goal, ten minutes later, came from an amazing show of determination. Taking a long ball from Kev he drove through the Flyers' midfield but finding the defenders bearing down on him he slid the ball to Tasha. She slotted it back immediately as the defenders came for her and Danny hammered it home, well beyond the keeper's reach.

The game finished with the score at 3–0. As the Dale Valley supporters broke on to the pitch Tasha leaned forward and kissed Danny on the cheek. 'You said we'd bury 'em,' she grinned.

On Monday most of the gang were playing table-tennis when Mr Blinks came into the room.

'This is it,' said Rachel to Danny. 'He's mad. He's closing us down.'

But Mr Blinks went over to Tasha. 'I've heard about you,' he said. 'You're our new top striker. Congratulations!'

He turned to Rachel. 'You're quite a player, too, I hear. I've just been telling Terry, it's time we had girls in the team.'

He raised his voice to speak to the gang. 'You know that Sidney and I were tricked into going to Bigley television studio on Saturday. But, no problem. We met the Desert Winds, the group at the top of the charts. Sidney's decided to give up football and learn the guitar. Show them your new gear, son.'

Sidney came into the room; purple trousers, a cream silk shirt and a guitar as big as himself.

'You know,' said Tasha to Rachel. 'I almost feel sorry for him. I'm glad my dad's not a millionaire.'

Seeing Red

Alan Durant

You know that feeling you get when they're doing the FA Cup draw on the telly and you're waiting for the ball with your team's number to be picked out? That nervy mixture of butterflies-in-the-stomach and excitement? Well, that's the way it was at Grafton Park's training session that Tuesday evening when the coach, Bill Davies, called the team together to announce who they were going to play in the quarter finals of the District Cup.

'Right,' said Bill. 'I know you're all dying to know who your next cup opponents will be.' His statement was met by a breathless hubbub. 'What do you want first: the good news or the bad news?'

'The good news!' Jamie Lewis responded quickly with the authority of the team captain that he was.

'Yes, the good news,' agreed Shanta, the team's star player, and other voices supported him.

'Okay,' said Bill, a smile on his round, healthily ruddy face. 'We'll be playing at home.'

'Yes!' cheered the team as one.

'And the bad news ...' Bill's smile became a grimace. 'We've been drawn against Barton.'

The response this time was more varied. Some groaned, some shrugged and one, Shanta, stood completely silent and still. When Jamie Lewis, who was standing next to him, turned towards his friend, Shanta's face was grim. It was as if he'd just heard that someone had died or something, not a cup draw.

'It'll be okay, Shanta,' Jamie said quietly. He put his hand on Shanta's shoulder. But Shanta shrugged it away.

'Barton,' he muttered glumly. 'Why of all teams did it have to be Barton?' He kicked up a divot of turf from the ground. Then, without another word, he turned and walked away.

It had been an excellent season so far for Grafton. They were currently top of their league, having won all but three of their matches, two of which had been drawn. Their only defeat had come at home and the team that had inflicted it upon them was Barton Green. The score had been 2–0, but the result told only half the story. For Shanta, the game had been a nightmare. Man marked throughout by a boy called Darren Powell, Shanta had hardly got a kick all match – well, a kick of the ball anyway; he'd had plenty of kicks on the legs and ankles, as well as jabs and shoves in the back, and all kinds of nasty threats and insults snarled in his ear. He'd come out of the game black and blue all over. But his tormentor had gone unpunished. Darren Powell was a thug but he was cunning too and had always committed his fouls on Shanta when the referee wasn't looking. A couple of times Shanta had complained, but the referee told him to get on with the game and stop moaning.

Finally, Shanta's temper had snapped. Reacting to a particularly painful dig in the ribs, Shanta had lashed out with his arm and caught Darren Powell full in the face with his elbow. Darren Powell had fallen to the ground as if shot. When Shanta turned, he saw his tormentor writhing on the ground with his hands over his face – and they were covered in blood. It had looked worse than it really was – Darren Powell just had a bleeding nose – but unfortunately for Shanta, on this occasion the referee *had* been looking. Without hesitation, he had reached into his pocket and shown Shanta the red card.

'Go on,' he'd said sternly. 'I've had enough of you. Get off.'

Shanta had raised his hands to protest, but, well, what could he say? Miserably, he'd trudged off the pitch and back to the changing rooms.

The score at the time had been nil all. But with almost all of the second half to go, Barton made their extra man count, netting two goals late in the game to win the match and deepen Shanta's misery. Most of his team-mates had witnessed Darren Powell's vicious tactics and after the match they were very sympathetic. No one blamed him for the loss. But Shanta blamed himself. He was angry and ashamed and very unhappy. He was in tears all the way home. Worse was to follow, though. Following the referee's report, the league organisers had charged Shanta with violent conduct and banned him for the rest of the season. Shanta was devastated, but Bill Davies had sent a letter appealing against the decision, and a number of spectators who had been at the match had supported him. The ban had been changed to three matches, but with a warning that if Shanta were sent off again, he would be banned from playing in the league for ever. Now Grafton had drawn Barton Green in the cup quarter finals, and, in the first game back after suspension, Shanta would have to face Darren Powell. No wonder he was feeling glum!

The evening after Bill Davies announced the draw, the Grafton Park coach turned up unexpectedly at Shanta's house.

'Sorry to disturb you, Mrs Nawaz,' he said with an apologetic smile. 'I just needed to have a little chat with Shanta about the match on Saturday. I expect he's told you we're playing Barton.'

Mrs Nawaz beckoned Bill Davies in. 'He's not said a word,' she said. 'He's been quiet as the grave since he got home last night. Now I know why.' She shook her head knowingly, then called upstairs to Shanta to come down.

'I'll leave you two to it,' she said when her son appeared, frowning, at the top of the stairs.

'Thanks,' said Bill. 'We won't be long.'

Shanta sat opposite his coach with a forlorn expression on his face.

'Cheer up,' Bill chided. 'You've got a cup quarter final on Saturday to look forward to.'

'Yes,' Shanta mumbled. 'Against Barton. And Darren Powell.'

'So?' the coach persisted. 'Barton are nothing special and Darren Powell's just a thug.'

'I know,' Shanta grumbled. 'I've still got a couple of bruises from last time we played.'

'You're not worried about a couple of bruises, are you?' said Bill lightly.

'No,' said Shanta.

'What is the matter, then?' asked Bill. 'Are you scared of Darren Powell? Is that it?'

Shanta snorted. 'Of course I'm not scared of him,' he rasped angrily. 'I'd stand up to that creep any day. I'd ...' He cut himself short, glancing guiltily at his raised fist.

'That's what I was afraid of,' sighed Bill. He looked at the boy with unusual severity. 'If you can't control your temper, Shanta, then I can't risk playing you. This match means too much to the team. I know what an important player you are – heaven knows we've missed you these last few games – but I think I'm going to have to leave you out of this one – for your own good and the team's.'

'No,' cried Shanta. 'You can't do that.'

'I can and I will,' said Bill firmly. His gaze softened a little. 'Look, Shanta, you're a very talented lad. You don't want to ruin your whole football career before it gets started for the sake of one football match – even if it is a quarter final. There'll be other quarter finals – and semi-finals, and finals too, hopefully. Why not give this one a miss?'

He looked searchingly at his young striker. It would be so easy to agree, thought Shanta – to drop out of this one; the team would still have a good chance of winning without him. And if they didn't, no one would blame him, would they? *Oh, yes they would*, a voice in his head replied. *You would blame yourself.*

Shanta looked down at the floor. 'I want to play,' he said softly. Then, lifting his head so that he was staring straight into the coach's keen blue eyes, he added beseechingly, 'Please.'

For several moments, the room was tensely silent, while Bill Davies contemplated the dilemma that faced him. Then, at last, his features relaxed into a half smile and he nodded. 'Okay, you're in. But,' he warned, 'one hint of trouble and I'm taking you off. Understood?'

'I won't make any trouble,' Shanta promised. Then he smiled for the first time that day. 'Well, except for the Barton defence. I'll give them plenty of trouble – trying to stop me scoring ...'

'That's the spirit,' said Bill Davies happily. 'Let your skill do the talking, not your fists.'

'Barton Green won't know what's hit them,' said Shanta and his smile broadened into a grin.

A few days later, lining up for the kick-off with Barton Green and seeing Darren Powell waiting for him, Shanta didn't feel quite so confident. He felt unusually nervous: he was excited about the game, yet almost wished it was over. And it didn't take long for Darren Powell to make his mark. The match was only minutes old when the Barton defender gave Shanta a sharp tap on the ankle that made him hop up in pain – but out of the referee's view of course.

'That's for last time,' Darren Powell hissed. 'No one hits me and gets away with it. You're really going to get it now.'

He nudged Shanta in the back, pushing him forward. Shanta stumbled then turned with a glare at his marker. His face was hot with anger.

'I'm not scared of you,' he said fiercely. He would have said more too, only he suddenly remembered Bill Davies's words. Glancing across at the touchline Shanta could see the coach staring across at him and the heavy frown on his face. Quickly, he moved away. It was fortunate that he did, too, because at that moment Jamie Lewis threaded a pass through towards him. Shanta took it and, finding himself in space for once, with Darren Powell metres away, he was able to turn and run at the Barton defence. In a flash he was past two flat-footed defenders and in the Barton penalty box. As the goalkeeper advanced to narrow the angle, Shanta dummied to shoot,

then rolled the ball sideways for Jamie Lewis to run
on to and thump first time into the back of the net.
Goal! Less than five minutes gone and Grafton were
one-nil up! Shanta was delighted. As he ran back to
the centre circle, he passed Darren Powell, who
scowled at him unpleasantly.

'That's the last touch of the ball you'll get,' he
snarled.

Shanta just grinned and said nothing. He didn't
need to. Well, his feet had done his talking for him,
hadn't they? He'd shown Darren Powell who was
boss.

'Great run, Shanta,' Jamie Lewis congratulated
him. 'Thanks for the pass. I thought you were going
to shoot yourself.'

'Well, maybe I will next time,' said Shanta happily. He'd get another chance soon, he was sure of
that.

But his confidence was misplaced. Darren Powell
may not have been the most skilful footballer on
the pitch, but he was a strong defender – and he was
as good as his word: for the rest of the first half,
Shanta hardly touched the ball. Every time a pass
was hit in his direction, Darren Powell intercepted it
or tackled Shanta before he had the chance to get
the space to move away. And in between times,
when the referee wasn't looking, he used his full
range of dirty tricks to try to hurt and provoke
Shanta. The names he called him were even nastier

now and Shanta was finding it more and more
difficult to control his temper. He was just a step
away from lashing out.

It wasn't just Shanta personally who was strug-
gling. After their glorious start, Grafton started to
lose their way and allow Barton back in the game. A
careless mistake in their defence let Barton's central
striker, Carl Hewitt, race clear to shoot home the
equaliser. Even worse, in his brave attempt to save
the goal, Grafton's keeper, Danny Marsden, landed
heavily and injured himself.

'I think he's dislocated his shoulder,' Bill Davies
announced glumly, as Danny was led away in tears
by one of the watching parents to be taken to
hospital. 'He certainly won't be taking any further
part in this match.'

Grafton had a substitute, Jermain Stewart, but he
wasn't a goalkeeper, so Bill Davies had to reorganise
the team. Shanta's fellow striker, Mark Bridges, the
tallest player in the side, went in goal and Jermain
took his place up front. It wasn't a happy arrange-
ment. With Shanta shackled by Darren Powell and
Grafton's midfield passing badly, Jermain was
unable to get into the game at all – while at the
back, Mark Bridges had a nightmare.

In the space of three minutes at the end of the
first half, Mark had let in two goals. The first, a
rocket of a shot from Barton's captain, Ben Smith,
wasn't his fault, but the second definitely was. Carl

Hewitt's soft header seemed to be bouncing harmlessly into the stand-in keeper's hands, but somehow, Mark Bridges let it slip through. To the horror of the watching Grafton players, the ball trickled over the line for a goal. At half-time Grafton were 3–1 down and staring defeat in the face.

Bill Davies was furious.

'Don't you want to get into the semi-final?' he stormed. 'You're throwing the game away.' Brusquely, he listed the many things the team was doing wrong. His most stinging remarks were saved for Shanta.

'It's no good just waiting for the ball to come to you, Shanta, and letting Darren Powell say "thank you very much" as he takes it off you,' said the coach severely. 'You've got to move about. Make space.'

'But how can I make space?' Shanta grumbled. 'Everywhere I go, Darren Powell follows. Look at my legs.' He rolled down the sock on his right leg to reveal a collection of bruises.

Bill Davies shook his head. 'If I had another substitute I'd take you off,' he said. 'But I don't.' He gave Shanta a searching look. 'But if you really haven't got the stomach to cope with a marker, then maybe you should swap with Mark and take his place in goal. Let's see how he gets on against Darren Powell.'

Mark Bridges' face lit up at this suggestion. After his error in the first-half, he had no wish to stay in goal. It was a tempting offer too, Shanta had to admit. He couldn't do worse than Mark had done and he'd be free of Darren Powell at last. But just at that instant, he caught a glimpse of the Barton boy, leering across at him triumphantly – and Shanta's anger rose. He couldn't let Darren Powell think he'd beaten him. He had to stay out on the field.

'I'll move about,' he said sharply. 'Darren Powell will have to run a marathon to stay with me.'

'Good,' said Bill Davies. 'Take him all over the field, test his stamina. And if you still can't shake him off, then come deeper, into your own half and let Jamie push on up front. I'll give you the sign. Okay?'

'Okay,' said Shanta. Then it was time to line up for the second-half.

As the Grafton players jogged to their positions, the coach put a hand on Shanta's arm. 'Remember, Shanta,' he said quietly, 'keep your anger in your feet. Hit Barton where it really hurts – in their goal.'

'I'll try,' Shanta promised. But trying wasn't enough, he knew: he had to succeed.

Grafton started the second half as they had the first, with some good, flowing attacks, going close to scoring on two occasions. Then, at last, they got their reward when Jamie Lewis tapped in his second goal following a corner. Shanta, however, still couldn't get into the game. He moved from wing to wing to try and find space, but he couldn't shake off his marker. All he got for his trouble were a couple more bruises. Darren Powell was starting to breath quite heavily now, though, and no longer had the puff to utter his insults, which encouraged Shanta to carry on with his running.

'I've got you now,' he said to himself.

But Darren Powell was nothing if not determined. His breathing got more and more laboured yet he wouldn't let Shanta escape his clutches – and his off-the-ball tricks got more vicious. As Grafton attacked down their right side, Shanta moved to sprint towards the centre from the position he'd taken up out on the left wing. He'd barely taken two steps, though, when his legs were swept from under him and he collapsed to the ground.

'Ah!' he cried, clutching his left ankle, which had twisted in the fall.

'Had a nice trip?' sneered Darren Powell, standing over him. The Barton boy's taunting words and expression made Shanta see red. A jolt of anger surged through him.

'You dirty thug!' he hissed, lifting his foot to kick out … It was the sound of his coach's voice, calling from the nearby touch-line, that stopped him. Shanta dropped his leg and, gingerly, got up on his feet.

'Shanta!' Bill Davies called again. Glancing aside, Shanta saw his coach jerk a thumb in the direction of the Grafton half. Shanta nodded, then, limping slightly, he trotted away from his marker, who watched him with a look of hard satisfaction. This time, he didn't bother trying to follow.

There were barely ten minutes of the match left now. Grafton were trying hard, but their early second-half pressure had eased through tiredness. The Barton players were weary too but they kept on battling with everyone back behind the ball. Only something special, it seemed, could unlock their defence – and Shanta was the one to provide it. Taking the ball from Mark Bridges, deep in his own half, he sprinted forward. As a man, the Barton side fell back before him and he was able to get half-way into his opponents' half before someone came to challenge him. Shanta swerved past him and quickly eased by a second tackle too. There were still plenty of Barton players between him and the goal, though.

As Shanta looked up to see who was free in front of him, Jamie Lewis made a darting run across the penalty box towards him. Shanta shaped as if to pass to him, but held on to the ball instead, moving inside towards the Barton goal. Two Barton defenders had gone with Jamie Lewis, expecting him to get the ball and, now, suddenly, a gap had opened in the heart of the Barton defence. Shanta needed no second invitation. Quick as a flash, he was through the gap and bearing down on the Barton goal. Unsure whether to come or stay, the Barton keeper dithered and by the time he'd made up his mind to advance it was too late. Shanta had slipped the ball

past him and into the corner of the net. Grafton
had equalised! It was 3–3. Shanta slid to the ground
in delight, as his team-mates ran to congratulate
him.

'Great goal, son!' Bill Davies shouted from the
touchline, his round face ruddier than ever. 'Now,
let's have another one!'

Shanta did his best to oblige. In the next few
minutes he got more good touches of the ball than
he'd had in the whole game up till then. Twice he
set up clear chances for his team-mates with clever
runs and passes, but each time they failed to make
them count. As if gathering confidence from their
good fortune, Barton mounted one last attack and
won a corner. As he trotted over to take the kick,
Ben Smith waved his team-mates forward. The
Grafton penalty area was a mass of Barton green and
Grafton blue. Only the Barton goalkeeper remained
in his own half of the field. The kick came over.
Jarmain Stewart got his head to the ball but only
knocked it up in the air. Darren Powell leapt high
and headed the ball back hopefully towards the
Grafton goal – and there was Carl Hewitt unmarked,
on the edge of the six-yard box! It seemed that he
must score ... But no! Bravely, Mark Bridges flung
himself forward to smother the ball just as the
striker was about to shoot.

'Brilliant save!' cried Jamie Lewis. While all eyes
turned towards the Barton goalkeeper, Shanta made
his move.

'Mark!' he shouted. 'Kick it!' Then he turned and ran upfield. Mark Bridges' kick was a good one. Making full use of his striker's skills, he thumped the ball well into the Barton half. Shanta was away. His first touch, though, took him a little to one side of the field and by the time he'd got the ball under control and got back on course, he was aware of a figure snapping at his heels. Somehow he knew at once, even without seeing him, who it was: Darren Powell. Shanta accelerated forward, making sure he didn't push the ball too far ahead of him. Darren Powell followed doggedly. He may have been tired but he wasn't going to let his quarry go free.

Shanta was in the penalty area now, the Barton keeper coming out to meet him. Darren Powell was at his shoulder. Should he shoot now, even though the angle was bad, and hope for the best, or . . ? He stopped and swivelled with the ball. Darren Powell was completely fooled. He ran right past Shanta, who came back inside and advanced on the goal. A shimmy left, then right and the keeper was out of it, lying helplessly on the turf. The goal was at Shanta's mercy. He pulled back his foot to tap home the ball and whack! For the second time in the match his legs were swept from under him by Darren Powell. This time, though, the incident had happened in full view of the referee. Instantly, he blew his whistle and pointed to the penalty spot. Then, beckoning to Darren Powell with one hand, he reached into his pocket with the other. Picking himself up, Shanta watched as Darren Powell was shown the red card and sent from the pitch.

'That'll teach him, dirty fouler,' Jermain muttered. 'He should have been off ages ago.'

Shanta said nothing. The job was not yet complete. Coolly, he picked up the ball and placed it on the penalty spot. Then he turned and took a few steps back. The Barton keeper swayed nervously on his line. The whistle blew. Shanta stood motionless for an instant, then trotted forward and thump! The ball was in the net. 4–3! Grafton had beaten Barton with the last kick of the quarter final! As his teammates leapt and whooped for joy, Shanta looked across to the changing rooms, into which Darren Powell was about to disappear, and he raised a fist in the air. Returning his gaze to the pitch, all he could see was the rush of blue that swiftly enveloped him.

Tanner's Ace

Peter Dixon

Jason placed his Inter-Milano sports bag on the spare seat and settled down for the drive to Fern End Middle School. He knew they had a poor side and looked forward to scoring his third hat-trick of the season. Being captain he swiftly bagged the front seat, and hoped that Thalia Mansell would notice the scarlet Inter-Milano shirt draped across his shoulders. No one else possessed a Milan shirt, and no one else had a photograph of themselves scoring the winning goal for the district side.

He slipped the picture from the back page of the gazette into his hand and gazed at it once again. Surely Thalia must have seen it? Perhaps she had even cut it out and pinned it to her wall. His head spun at the thought. Thalia, the best-looking girl in the school – perhaps she really had cut out her own copy. He reread the caption printed in large, fat, black letters:

TANNER'S ACE
Local boy

He didn't want to grin but couldn't quite help it. Tanner's ace. Yes, that's what he was – an ace. The best sportsman in the school.

Even at the pre-school playgroup he had won more races than anyone else, and this success had continued throughout his infant and junior years.

Now, aged eleven, he was still winning just about everything he entered, and if it hadn't been for stupid Porky Day he would have won the young Athlete of the Year award at the area sports. Stupid, giggling, silly Porky Day who had tripped him at the very first bend of the 400 metres, and even Jason couldn't win a race with only one shoe and a bleeding knee. Stupid, bloomin' Porky Day, tripping someone up was typical of him. Just the sort of daft thing he would do. Jason turned his head towards the back seat where Porky and Mickey Iddon were wrestling each other. Porky had pulled his football bag over Iddon's head, and Iddon had trapped Porky's head between his elbow and the back of the seat. There were a lot of muffled hissings and groanings, mixed with outbursts of giggles and grunts. Their battle was attracting considerable attention and with some dismay, Jason noticed that Thalia and some of the other girls seemed to be enjoying the struggle and even encouraging the pair to wrestle harder.

For a moment Jason considered informing Mr Pike of the foolish behaviour in the back seat, but noticing the furrowed ridges of concentration upon their teacher's brow, he decided that perhaps it wasn't a wise move. Mr Pike needed all his concentration for the road. At least Thalia had decided to come and support the team and Jason secretly hoped that he was the main attraction. But whatever could she find amusing about Porky Day?

Porky was a twit and why had Mr Pike put him in the squad anyway, Jason wondered? He didn't even own a designer sports bag and in their previous match he had worn a pair of his brother's old army cadet boots. One of them seemed devoid of laces and every time Porky attempted a left-footed clearance, the boot flew off and sailed high into the air and he had to scramble after it.

And then there was the incident of the shredded shirt. Porky had snatched Iddon's number seven shirt from his bag in one of their usual struggles and thrown it into the caretaker's front garden. Before Mickey could retrieve it, Mr Lambercraft's basset hound and a mongrel which hung around the kitchens had torn it to shreds in a battle of snarls, snaps and writhing bodies. There was a terrible row. Mr Pike had ordered Porky to give his shirt to Mickey Iddon and poor Porky had had to play in his vest. It was a particularly nasty vest of a sort of fluffy ivory colour, but Porky didn't care and laughed as loudly as anyone else when Frankie Burrows pointed out huge holes down the side and the massive brown iron stain in the middle of the back.

The thought of playing in a grandfather vest in front of fifty supporters including the glorious Thalia filled Jason with sickening horror, but Porky hadn't cared a jot. It was in that same match that Iddon and Porky had used some of the half-time orange peel to make themselves goofy teeth and upset the referee. Jason had reported them to Mr

Pike, who in turn relegated them to the role of substitutes for the next two games.

'Football is a serious game and a pitch is no place for fooling,' Mr Pike had announced. Jason had felt pleased. He was secretly delighted to know that they wouldn't be starting the match today.

The mini-bus gave a lurch as it negotiated two linked roundabouts, and Jason's new bag slipped sideways. He stared at it with pleasure. No one else in the entire county owned a scarlet Inter-Milano bag, it was unique.

Yet he remembered, not for the first time, that this wasn't true: Glenda had one. Silly, squealy Glenda. She had one and to Jason it didn't seem fair. It was bad enough having a nearly six foot elder sister, but her ownership of an Inter-Milano sports bag was impossible for Jason to accept.

When their Uncle Derek had visited the factory in Italy where they were made, he had brought two back. Why two? One bag would have been perfect Why hadn't he brought Glenda something different? She didn't even play football, in fact she didn't play anything much. Majorettes, that was her thing, and every time Jason observed her folding her white skirt, blouse, knickers and bra into a soft little bundle and placing them in her bag with an assortment of lucky koala bears, pretty towels and stepping boots, he wanted to scream. Inter-Milano bags were not designed for sisters who marched round in high stepping parades of long legs, batons

and swirling skirts, they were for football stars.
People such as himself and other guys. Every time
Jason saw her bag he felt like kicking it as far as ...

There was a scream! It was followed by a cry from
Thalia, and Mr Pike hit the brakes. It was Iddon's
voice trumpeting through the mini-bus.

'It's Perkins, sir. Perkins is being sick, sir. Perkins is
being sick all over!' And so he was. Perkins stood
grey as sugar paper amidst a host of scrabbling
travellers and tumbling sports bags, spurting a
deluge of pink froth.

'It's sherbet!' screamed Julie Davis, trying to hide
beneath her seat. 'It's sherbet sick.'

Amidst the shrieking and chaos, Jason fought to
drag his bag from Perkins's range but it was too late.

Then as suddenly as he started, Perkins stopped.
For a moment he looked vaguely puzzled and then
he sat down and wiped his mouth on his cuff.

'It was Porky Day who done it,' shouted Neil. 'Me
and Thalia heard him daring Perkins to eat those
five packets all at once. He said he'd give him a set
of England cards if he did,' he added. There was a
further silence, even the road was empty and quiet.

'Everyone out,' snapped Mr Pike,' and keep away
from the road.'

They sat on a low white wall which surrounded
the garden of a big posh house, whilst Mr Pike
dished out wads of green paper towels and people
dabbed each other off. It was horrible. Jason's Inter-
Milano bag seemed to have caught the worst of the

mess and he was moaning and groaning whilst attempting to remove the foaming fluid with half a packet of green paper towels. Only Perkins seemed at all cheerful and wandered around with a smile telling everyone how much better he felt.

Mr Pike was obviously terribly angry and had begun making an announcement about telephoning the school, when Danny La Rocca appeared. Mr Pike noticed the man as he waved from the gravel path leading to the double garage, nosed by a bright silver sports car and a Mercedes. For a moment he thought it was a grumpy rich man complaining about schoolchildren sitting on his wall.

He couldn't have been more wrong! As the bronzed figure strode forward Iddon gave a whoop of recognition. It was Rovers' leading goal scorer and international superstar, Danny La Rocca himself! The class fell into silence. Jason ceased dabbing his bag, and even Mr Pike looked embarrassed and tongue-tied. It didn't matter, though, for Danny had everything under control.

At a glance, he noted the array of football gear, Perkins clutching the yellow bucket and Jason still dabbing his bag. Danny groaned. He was bigger, browner and even more wonderful than anyone ever imagined. He had a tattoo on the hairy part of his wrist and a gold medallion around his neck.

'It happens to the best of us,' he laughed, patting Perkins' head. 'But where are you off to?'

'Fern End School,' Mr Pike replied. 'Can we use your phone – I'll have to cancel.'

'Cancel!' roared Danny, his gold filling glinting. 'Cancel! We don't cancel matches as important as yours, do we Jack?'

A small man holding a rake had appeared at his side. Danny looked at his watch.

'Fern End School's five miles from here. I'll drive ahead and tell them you're delayed and when you've cleaned things up a bit you can drive on.'

Mr Pike opened his mouth and shut it again.

'Well, who's coming in the advance party with me?' Danny grinned.

Of course, everyone wanted to say 'Me.' The idea of driving into Fern End School with Danny La Rocca in a sports car was a dream come true – yet only Jason spoke.

'I'll come,' he said very coolly. 'I'm the captain and I know the way.'

'And me!' cried Porky Day. 'I'll sit in the back.'

He moved towards the driveway, but Jason moved faster.

'No, not you, Porky! I think one of the girls. How about Thalia?'

'Okay, one of each sounds about right' said Danny, laughing, and he vaulted the garden gate and trotted towards the car.

The moment the sports car swept into the Fern End School playground with Jason seated beside Danny La Rocca was the greatest moment of his eleven and a half years. Thalia's hair had blown in the breeze for the entire journey and on one occasion she had leaned so far forward that their cheek's had almost touched. Jason had half-turned – grinned, and sensed that she had enjoyed the contact as much as he had himself.

Within minutes Danny La Rocca was recognised. News sped through the school and a crowd of Lower Juniors followed the trio towards the pitch, waving, pointing and chanting the Rovers' song. Danny grinned and Jason waved. They explained the situation to the Fern End School's teacher who understood the dilemma and agreed to postpone the kick-off for a short while, and then when Danny agreed to stay and watch the match for a few minutes, the day was completed.

'Perhaps you'd like me to be photographed shaking hands with the two captains,' he suggested.

Thalia laughed and asked if he could also play on her side.

'We could chuck out Iddon and have a decent striker,' joked Jason, throwing his arm across Thalia's shoulder and beaming to all those standing near. The time flew as magic minutes always do, and suddenly Jason realised that his team were trotting on to the pitch, having changed in the mini-bus.

A moment of panic struck him. 'My bag! Quick! I must change! Where's my bag?'

'You left it on the wall,' said Mr Pike rather grumpily. 'But don't worry, we brought it for you.'

Without a word Jason grabbed the bag and fled to the changing room. He tore off his shoes, socks, jacket and shirt and unzipped the chrome Inter-Milano double-way siliconed zipper. He pulled away the towel covering the kit and stared down. A pair of neatly folded knickers, a bra, blouse and silver-tipped majorette cane stared back.

'Hurry up!' called Mr Pike. 'The *Gazette* want a picture of you shaking hands with Mr La Rocca!'

dolphin story collections

chosen by Wendy Cooling

1 top secret
stories to keep you guessing by Rachel Anderson, Andrew
Matthews, Jean Richardson, Leon Rosselson, Hazel Townson and
Jean Ure

2 on the run
stories of growing up by Melvin Burgess, Josephine Feeney,
Alan Gibbons, Kate Petty, Chris Powling and Sue Vyner

3 aliens to earth
stories of strange visitors by Eric Brown, Douglas Hill,
Helen Johnson, Hazel Townson and Sue Welford

4 go for goal
soccer stories by Alan Brown, Alan Durant, Alan Gibbons,
Michael Hardcastle and Alan MacDonald

5 wild and free
animal stories by Rachel Anderson, Geoffrey Malone, Elizabeth
Pewsey, Diana Pullein-Thompson, Mary Rayner and Gordon Snell

6 weird and wonderful
stories of the unexpected by Richard Brassey, John Gatehouse,
Adèle Geras, Alison Leonard, Helen McCann and Hazel Townson

7 timewatch
stories of past and future by Stephen Bowkett, Paul Bright, Alan
MacDonald, Jean Richardson, Francesca Simon and Valerie Thame

8 stars in your eyes
stories of hopes and dreams by Karen Hayes, Geraldine Kaye,
Jill Parkin, Jean Richardson and Jean Ure

9 spine chillers
ghost stories by Angela Bull, Marjorie Darke, Mal Lewis Jones,
▓er Stevens, Hazel Townson and John West